Superphonics® *Storybooks* **will help your child to learn to read using Ruth Miskin's highly effective phonic method. Each story is fun to read and has been carefully written to include particular sounds and spellings.**

The Storybooks are graded so your child can progress with confidence from easy words to harder ones. There are four levels - Blue (the easiest), Green, Purple and Turquoise (the hardest). Each level is linked to one of the core *Superphonics® Books.*

ISBN: 978 0 340 77350 5

Text copyright © 2002 Gill Munton
Illustrations copyright © 2002 Steve Cox

Editorial by Gill Munton
Design by Sarah Borny

The rights of Gill Munton and Steve Cox to be identified as the author and illustrator of this Work have been asserted by them in accordance with the Copyright, Designs and Patents Act 1988.

First published in Great Britain 2002

10 9 8 7 6 5

First published in 2002 by Hodder Children's Books, a division of Hachette Children's Books, 338 Euston Road, London NW1 3BH
An Hachette UK Company. www.hachette.co.uk

Printed and bound in China by WKT Company Ltd.

A CIP record is registered by and held at the British Library.

Target words

All the Blue Storybooks focus on the following sounds:

a as in **cat** | **e** as in **wet**
i as in **bin** | **o** as in **fox**
u as in **bug** |

These target words are featured in the book:

at	Tag	big	box	bug
bath	van	bin	fog	bus
cat(s)		dish	fox	fun
fat	bed	fish	hot	hut
hat	den	his	log	Mum
lap	get	in	lot(s)	pup
Mag	hen	Jim	Mog	rug
man	Jem	Sim	nod	shut
map	Ned	sit	on	sun
mat	net	Tig	pop	us
nap	Red	tin	pot	yum
path	shed	with	shop	
Sam	wet			

Other words

Also included are some common words (e.g. **and**, **go**) which your child will be learning in his or her first few years at school.

A few other words have been used to help the stories to flow.

Reading the book

1 Make sure you and your child are sitting in a quiet, comfortable place.

2 Tell him or her a little about the stories, without giving too much away:

In the first story, a naughty dog gets even naughtier!

In the second story, a little boy and his mother try to get on a very full bus.

In the last story, Nat the rat steals some food belonging to a cat - but he doesn't get away with it!

This will give your child a mental picture; having a context for a story makes it easier to read the words.

3 Read the target words (above) together. This will mean that you can both enjoy the stories without having to spend too much time working out the words. Help your child to sound out each word (e.g. **c-a-t**) before saying the whole word.

4 Let your child read each of the stories aloud. Help him or her with any difficult words and discuss the story as you go along. Stop now and again to ask your child to predict what will happen next. This will help you to see whether he or she has understood what has happened so far.

Above all, enjoy the stories, and praise your child's reading!

Ruth Miskin's
Superphonics®
Blue Storybook

Bad Dog!

by Gill Munton

Illustrated by Steve Cox

Hodder
Children's
Books

a division of Hachette Children's Books

Ben is
a bad dog.

Look at him! **Yap!**
Yap!

"Bad dog!"

Look at him!

Yum!
Yum!

"Bad dog!"

Look at him!

Rip!
Rip!

"Bad dog!"

6

Ben is a bad dog.

But he's my dog!

On the bus

There's a man with a fan
and a big red pan

On the bus.

There's a chap in a cap
with a pig on his lap

On the bus.

There's a rat in a hat
and a big fat cat

On the bus.

There are ten thin men
and a fox ... and a hen

On the bus.

There are six sad dogs
and a box of logs

On the bus.

There's a goat called Gus ...

There's no room for us
On the bus!

Tom's got a tin
that he puts things in:

A pen, and some gum,
and a bus, and a pin ...

A bag of sweets,
and some nuts,
and a fox ...

A banana and a bun,
and a little red box.

But Nat likes nuts and
Nat likes buns!

He gets in the tin ...
and then out he comes!

In go the nuts,
and in goes the bun.

"Now for that banana -
Tom's tin is fun!"

In goes the banana
(all but the skin).

Not much food left
in Tom's red tin!

And not much left
of the banana, nuts and bun!

Time to go, Nat ...
run, run, run!

Up gets Tom
and off runs Nat.

Tom runs after him ...
but look on the mat!

Down goes Tom ...
    and up goes Nat!

"Good!" nods Nat.
"I got away with that!"

Up gets Tom,
and sits on the mat.

And when Nat comes
down again ...

A tin full of rat!